For Daniel Grahamshire,
The Two-Toed King.

DRAMATIS PERSONAE

The House of Karanír

The House of Karanír can trace their descent to the old times, before the Ebonide King built his Great City. They are known for the bond they share with their famed Kúnadi.

Under the Ebonide King they served as scouts and huntsman. They were not among the noble houses who rebelled against the Ebonide King and sought him slain, yet some say, it was the Kúnadi that dealt the final blow.

Since the fall of Gordinal, they have returned to their homeland Dalkyr to the west.

Madog Karanír, Lord of Dalkyr, terribly ill and dying.
Ederys, his wife, Lady of Dalkyr
Prydonír, his son and heir
Rhodris, his middle son
Jádyn, his youngest son,
Elyssa, his only daughter

Worlyn, a druid from Kaer Dúsír
Toryg, a veteran Kúnadman
Malíkhar, Prydonír's Kúnadi
Vórgarys, Rhodris's Kúnadi
Namorys, Madog's Kúnadi
Hywel, an old Guardsman
Ouric, a young Guardsman

The House of Múran

Known as the Náedar Lords, the Múrans are master seafarers and traders. They were among the noble houses to turn on the Ebonide King during the rebellion. Their home is the island of Bren Yndal.

Llyros Múran, Lord of Bren Yndal, called the Lord of Náedaríad
Penárddys, his wife & Lady, daughter of the Ebonide King
Brenyn, his eldest son, a large boy of three years
Aradyn, his second son, a twin boy of one years
Páthos, his third son, a twin boy of one year
Skáthys, a Sworn Sword
Kabad, a Warrior Priest
Felymír, the Lord's bard

The House of Llúvelyn

The noble house of Llúvelyn have ruled the lands of Tenalír for at least two hundred years. Known as great administrators, the Llúveyn's are schooled from a young age to be both scholars and wise rulers.

Armon Llúvelyn, Lord of Tenalír, the Wisdom of the Tower
Telyth, his eldest daughter, married to the Lord of Bren Yndal
Áenon, his son and heir
Marwen, his younger daughter
Ortháel, Captain of the Custodians
Gáelan, a Custodian and Sworn Protector of the Lord

THE GHOSTS OF LLÍAN

The Silk Tapestry: Book One
Verse I

R.K. SIMONS

PROLOGUE

995th Year After Landing
285th Year of the Ebonide Kings

**The Great City of Gordinal,
Autumn**

The Ebonide King lay dead beneath the Sacred Tree, its ancient, crooked branches swaying in the night's breeze. The blood of the cruel despot pooled and streamed between the cracked joints of the Great Hall's stone floor.

Two pink blossoms shed free and descended from above. They settled around the dead king and sailed upon the crimson rivers that had spilled from several savage wounds.

A leather boot disturbed the grim scene, followed by a scarred hand, reaching down to pluck one of the blossoms from its bloody voyage.

'So, it is done then,' the bearded warrior inspected the blood-soaked flower for but a moment, before he turned to the armoured lord who loomed over the sodden body, a stained sword in hand and a panting silver Kúnadi at his side.

The Kúnadman did not reply. He remained silent, staring down at the slain king.

Judging by the king's features, now a ravaged hunk of torn flesh, his jaw hanging horribly loose, the Kúnadi had certainly had his share of the kill. But it was the bloody blade, dripping at the point, that revealed the true regicidal.

Lord Euros Múran discarded the pink blossom, casting it to the cold stone and approached the Kúnadman. 'Your men turned the tide, Madog, we would not have won this day without your aid. The just thing is done. The man was a tyrant.'

Madog Karanír met his eyes, his voice low. 'He was not always so.'

'No man is born evil. But a man does inherit a choice, a choice to choose his own path, and whatever path that man elects to tread will be the measure of him,' Euros said. 'This king chose a dark path indeed, and now he has paid the toll. We are on the right side of history, do not punish yourself for the path *you* have chosen this night. It was the right path, Madog, you may walk it with your head held high.'

Footfalls approached then, and several warriors entered the Great Hall, swords drawn, followed by Armon Llúvelyn, Lord of Tenalír, his blue cloak snapping as he strode through the hall's archway. Each of his warriors wore the strain of fatigue. The siege had lasted for almost a month, and hundreds, maybe thousands, had died. They had lost comrades, and no doubt they had come to the hall seeking vengeance for the fallen.

Three lords had rebelled against the Ebonide King, and the men of Tenalír, Gwynvór and Bren Yndal had laid siege to the great city. But it was only when a fourth lord elected to join their cause, had victory become attainable. The loyalist Kúnadmen of Dalkyr, it seemed, had turned on their master, and it was *they* who had dealt the vengeance for the Mad Monarchy's atrocities.

Euros turned to greet the Lord of Tenalír, and by the scowl that threatened to engulf the lord's sunken eyes and hooked nose, it was clear the man was in a severely foul mood and was hardly pleased with the gruesome scene he found before him.

Armon looked down at the bloody king and then to Euros. 'So, you have your justice do you, Náedaríad? Is this what the Lords of Bren Yndal deem a fitting end for a king? Bloodied upon the stones of his own Great Hall, beneath the Sacred Tree no less.'

Before Euros could retort, the Lord of Káer Kyral growled, and Madog spoke. 'It was a Kúnadman who dealt this justice, Lord.'

Lord Armon sneered at the words. 'Yes, not so loyal after all it seems. Where are the children?'

Euros saw Madog tense and the grip around the bloody blade tighten.

'You will not have the children.'

Armon's hooked nose arose, and he paused in thought before speaking calmly, 'I understand your feelings towards the children, Madog, and I want you to listen to me carefully... I am not a callous man, despite what some might say. I have children of my own, and I feel deeply for them. But this is no game.' He pointed a long finger down at the bloody body. 'What do you think they will do when they are grown? Forget that we murdered their father? Forgive us for our sins? Send the girl to the North by all means, but the boy cannot be allowed to live. You know this, for in his heart he shall always seek bloody vengeance for the slaying of his kin and the sacking of his home.'

Madog released a defeated sigh, and his head fell. Of course, Armon was right on the matter. It was too much of a risk for the young prince to live. Ten years from now the boy would be grown, and all he would need do is raise the banners of his House in the centre of any city of Hyráeth, and men would follow. Rebellion would come again to the lands, and anyone could spin a copper knot as to who would be victorious.

Euros, however, had other plans for the girl.

'I will take the princess,' he said, producing raised brows from both Armon and the Kúnadman. 'She will be betrothed to my heir. If her seed is of the line of Múran, how then will she have cause to sow rebellion.'

The Lord of Tenalír laughed mockingly. 'You seek a claim to the throne, Múran. How many times must I tell you to take me not as a fool.' The lord waved a bony hand. 'The girl will be sent to the mines of Gwynvór in the north.'

'Penarddys is a fragile girl,' Madog said. The man was visibly concerned, having watched over the prince and princess since they were babes. 'She would not survive the mines. I find Lord Múran's proposal more... acceptable.'

Lord Armon sighed and shook his head.

'Do not worry, friend,' Euros said, slapping the Lord of Tenalír on the back, unintentionally leaving a smear of dirt and blood upon the blue cloak. 'Who would you rather charge of the girl? On Bren Yndal she will be treated well, and any thought of revenge would soon be stripped away with the birth of a young Náedaríad. In Gwynvór, they breed beasts of fury, forge savage men and worship callous gods. It is no place for a forgotten princess.'

'Fine,' Armon agreed. 'I will compromise. You may take the girl to the Isle of the Náedar if you must. But the boy must die.'

Euros nodded. 'Agreed.'

'If it must be done,' Madog said. 'It is *I* who shall be the one. No other man will harm the boy. Is that clear?'

The Lord of Tenalír scowled at the Kúnadi Lord. 'You do not give orders here, Lord Karanír. It is I who-'

Euros turned to a low snarl that arose from one of the side entrances of the great hall. From the shadows between the pillars emerged a Kúnadi with thick silver fur and only one eye, a large Kúnadman stalked close behind.

More growls echoed into the hall then and Euros spun his head to the right. Several silver beasts were emerging from the shadows, with Dalkyr warriors at their backs, armed and eager for blood.

The Custodians of Tenalír moved to draw their blades, but a gesture from Armon halted their actions.

'You are mistaken, Lord Llúvelyn,' Madog said, wiping his blade and sheathing it. 'You are outnumbered by what? Four to one? More?' The Lord of the Kúnadi made a clicking noise and four warriors strode forward. 'My men will see to it that the King is given a proper burial, then I shall see to the prince.'

The burly Kúnadmen reached down and raised the dead king to their shoulders, the jaw sagged horribly as he was lifted, his eyes pale and vacant. Blood dripped to the floor as they respectfully removed the body from the hall.

'Very well,' Armon said, turning to his men. Euros thought for a moment he caught a sense of relief in the man. No doubt the responsibility of the war had weighed heavily on him. 'Secure the city!' The Lord of Tenalír yelled, and his men scurried from the hall. 'We shall return here on the morrow, lords, we have a realm to rebuild.'

The three lords nodded to one another and parted ways.

Beneath the swaying branches of the Sacred Tree, two pink blossoms, one cast away to cold stone, the other sailing a river of blood, bore witness, as the eternal tide turned once more.

PART ONE
THE HOUSE OF KARANÍR

"A tree with strong roots may endure the most violent storms."

CHAPTER ONE

1005th Year After Landing
10th Year of the Great Lords Period
Carnsday, 21st of Voydych

The Fortress of Kaer Kyral, Late Winter

Roiling waves crashed against the grey cliffs of the Dalkyr coast. A storm of fierce wind and wrathful thunder had battered the land for three days and nights. Submerged within the churning tempest, rising from the slick, wet rocks it was built upon, the fortress of Kaer Kyral stood silent and sombre, the Lord's Tower and outer walls periodically illuminated by sharp bursts of piercing lightning.

A lone light approached the ancient fortress from the east, shifting through dense forest that creaked and swayed beneath the looming regard of the tall tower. A figure emerged upon a pale horse from the undulating woodland and galloped for the eastern gate.

Two guards, clad in chainmail moved to open the gates as they spotted the rider, the light of a flickering lantern bobbing across the raised causeway that stretched across the wet sand and windswept beachgrass below.

'Get that portcullis up, Ouric!' the older guard ordered, wiping snot from his long, crooked nose. Shaking the rain from his brimmed helm, he pushed the younger lad towards the winch.

'Right away, sir!' Ouric said, an unwarranted enthusiasm to his youthful gait. The boy was keen to impress, still beaming with pride at having been chosen to man the castle walls, even on a night of unyielding, icy rain. The dark clouds that smothered the night sky were so dense, that not even the Arch of the World's celestial glow could breach them. The boy heaved and the chains pulled the latticed iron gate upwards.

'Good,' Huwel said. 'Now stand to attention and make yourself look official like.'

'Official, sir?'

'Eyes forward, boy, and hold your spear up like this.' Huwel held his spear to his side and stood as straight as he could. His back wasn't what it used to be, and he had a hard time getting up off his arse, let alone standing like a soldier. In cold weather he could hear his own spine creaking like an old oak.

Hooves pounded against cobbled ground as the rider charged into the courtyard. He rode a white cob, a sturdy mount bred for pulling carts. The horse spun around, and the rider swung from the saddle, dark robes snapping in the rain. The dark figure proceeded to unstrap an unusual staff from the off side of the horse. A misshapen thing with a gleaming orb on its end.

It had been some time since a druid had been approved entry to Kaer Kyral, and even longer since Huwel had laid eyes upon a Scholar of Dúsír. The last had been a miserable old bastard who had served House Karanir in the years before the rebellion. He had been younger then, when the druid had collapsed in the same courtyard, clutching his chest in agony. Nothing sinister had occurred of course, just the cruelty of time.

'The Lady awaits you, Master Druid!' Huwel yelled through the downpour. The rider turned to inspect them for a moment, his face hidden beneath a wide, gloomy cowl. He appeared to nod and spin away, his dark cloak trailing behind him, beating in the wind as he strode for the tower's main entrance.

'I've never seen a real druid before,' Ouric said, moving to stand beside the old warrior. 'My mother says that when the old king was slain, a thousand druids poured from every crack in the great city, like a deluge of filthy rats. She said they were exterminated after that, caught in traps laid by the Náedaríad.'

'Aye, some loyal to the King were killed, but it was the Priests of Mórnos who suffered the crueller fate,' Huwel said with a sigh. 'Drowned mostly. Stuffed into barrels and thrown from the cliffs, along with the king's family. Save for the princess of course.'

'Lady Penarddys?'

'That's the one. A pretty little thing. Slightly pale mind you. Might even catch a glimpse of her soon enough if you're lucky boy.'

'Really?'

'Oh aye. When the Master finally passes from this world, many lords and ladies will come to pay their respects to the Lord of the Kúnadi, the Hero of Gordinal.' Huwel looked the boy up and down. 'So, you best learn how to stand proper and hold your spear straight. Now, get that gate down and boil up some mussels and cockles in the pot will you! I'm cold and I'm bloody starving.'

Candles flickered as Lady Ederys guided the cloaked druid along the corridor that led to the Lord's Chamber. The walls of the passage were adorned with tapestries of long dead Kúnadi, loyal even after death.

She remembered years ago, when her father had dragged her kicking and screaming to Kaer Kyral, where she would be betrothed to a grubby young pup of House Karanír. Of course, beneath the sand and dirt, there was indeed a handsome young man to be found in Madog, albeit a gentle and foolishly brave man. And although the snarling Kúnadi woven into those ancient tapestries had once filled her with fear, over time, they had grown to become symbols of safety. For she knew now, there was no safer place than amongst a pack of loyal Kúnadi.

Behind her, the druid's staff clanked with every other step. His face had remained hidden beneath a dark hood, and his wet boots were leaving a trail of puddles in his wake. Ederys had been advised against inviting a Scholar of Dúsír to Kaer Kyral, the druids were still looked upon with a great deal of disdain by the peoples of Hyráeth, as many had knelt to the Ebonide King. Such an invitation was not without its risks.

Many lords of the realm still recalled the loyalty of House Karanír during the rebellion, who had remained at the king's side until the wrath of the people was at the foot of the Sacred Tree. If rumours were to spread of a druid at court, some may seek to question where the Kúnadmen's loyalty truly lay.

They reached the thick oak door, guarded by two Kúnadmen and their silver companions. The door was opened for them, and they entered.

Inside they found her sons and daughter, her young pups, stood about their father's deathbed, loyal guards each of them. The Lord's old Kúnadi Namorys was also present, laying at her master's feet. The old bitch growled as the druid past through the door. Though it may have been Rhodris, Ederys' second son, who in truth was more Kúnadi than boy, just like his grandfather.

The two youngest, Jádyn and Elyssa, looked up with wide eyes as the cloaked figure entered, especially Jádyn, who oft questioned his father on the Scholars of Dúsír and the Priests of Mórnos. Her eldest, Prydonír seemed less enthralled, but he respectfully bowed, nonetheless.

'If you could give us the room, my children. Our guest would see to your father,' Ederys requested.

The four pups understood their mother's tone and were quick to do as they were told, save for Rhodris who was reluctant to leave his father's side. But with a sharp look from his mother, the fiery pup soon followed his siblings. Not before, however, the boy released another low growl.

Ederys dared a glance at her husband then, which she was wont to do. It was difficult to look upon Madog like this, prone and helpless, sickly and pale, a shadow of the man he had once been. Ederys dreaded the thought of losing the true memory of him. Strong, tall, handsome, that is how she wanted to remember, not the sweating, gaunt figure that lay before her in this moment. The glance lasted little more than a second, but she could sense the picture seared into her memory, like a hot iron had branded her mind for evermore.

Only when the door was closed behind them did the druid deem it appropriate to drop the dark cowl and reveal his features. He was young, early twenties maybe, with a slender face and skin that was dyed with blue woad. He appeared blind in one eye, as the left was milky and scarred, useless it would seem. The other was green, and now regarded the pallid lord that lay before him.

'Can you heal him, Master Wórlyn?' Ederys asked, her heart racing.

The druid considered for a moment and knelt before the bed. Reaching over Madog, he opened the lord's tunic, and revealed a large, blackened abscess, that had appeared upon her husband's chest over a year ago.

'His illness is advanced,' the druid noted. 'You should have called for us sooner. I shall do what I can, but it does not look good.' He looked up at Ederys, she could no longer hold back the tears. 'I will need honey and rosemary, and a sharp, hot knife.'

She nodded and moved for the door.

'Do not allow the flower of hope to blossom, my Lady,' the druid warned. 'I fear it may well be too late.'

She left the room and did not look back.

An old sea shanty had joined the rumbling thunder and rain battered rocks below Kaer Kyral, rising and falling with each wave that crashed against the cliffs.

Young Ouric had never been known for his vocal range, but at least he knew the words, and in his mind that was all that mattered. He reached down and plucked a handful of mussels from a small gap in the rocks and dropped them into his bucket. Proud of himself, he continued to sing the old shanty he had learned from some island traders who had come through last summer...

On the winds I heard a priest's song
Heave the barrels, heave them
Oh, home is near, there's no need to fear
Heave the barrels, heave them
Onto the rocks, we'll pitch and swing
Heave the barrels, heave them
For home is near, there's no need to fear
So, heave the barrels, heave them
From deep below the priests will wail
Heave them barrels, heave them
For home is near, no need to fear
Heave the barrels, heave them
We slew the King beneath the tree
Heave the barrels, heave them

Oh...

A dark shape on the water's edge drew Ouric's attention. There was a small boat with a figure dragging it onto the sand. *Traders maybe?* he thought, although it was extremely late in the year for islanders, who were more like to visit during the summer or autumn. Regardless, he was keen to greet the newcomer, the trader may well come with tales of the endless seas, or, even better, another song to sing. Ouric grabbed his bucket, clambered down the slippery rocks with his bare feet, and eagerly pattered across the wet sand towards the figure.

'Hey there! You need a hand?' the boy called, nearing the boat. Though it was dark, Ouric could just about make out the trader. He was a tall, bald man with a long, black beard that fell to a point. There was a sparkle as the man turned, and Ouric noted the large rings that dangled from the man's earlobes, marking him as an islander. The trader wore thick furs and a dark leather tunic.

He smiled at Ouric, revealing a set of golden teeth. 'Aye, lad. I be trying to pull my boat up to that cave o'er there.' The man pointed to the other side of the beach.

'Ah, yes sir,' Ouric said enthusiastically, 'I know the one. I used to play in there with my friends when I was a boy. We used to pretend we were evil druids.'

The man chuckled. 'Is that so? Well, I am lucky I found you, lad.' He gestured to the front of the boat. 'If you could give us a pull, that would be grand.'

'Of course, sir,' Ouric said, moving to the front, searching for a rope. 'Happy to help. Say, you don't happen to know any sea shanties, do you? I learnt a new one a while back and it's-'

The wind whistled, and Ouric's rambling was cut short as a sharp pain ran through one side of his neck and out the other. Suddenly the world was upside down and there was sand in his hair. He saw a headless body fall to its knees and topple over before him. The trader, armed with a bloody cutlass, loomed over it.

Ouric garbled the words, '*heave the barrels, heave them,*' one last time, before his eyes rolled back into his skull, and he died.

CHAPTER TWO

The Fortress of Kaer Kyral,
Ádísday, 22nd of Voydych, 1005al

A flickering low light emanated from within the cave as Kabad thrust a handful of dried beach grass into the fire and warmed his cold, damp hands.

His vessel had been pulled inside with the aid of his newly raised headless servant, who now stood guard at the cave's entrance. The thrall's existence would be fleeting of course, so the ebonide priest stoked the fire once more before striding to the boat.

Kabad gathered the severed head of the boy, yanking the matted, blonde hair and placing it beside the snapping flames. The priest knelt before the lifeless face and began the ritual. Reaching inside his furs, he produced a handful of mooncap mushrooms, dropped them onto his tongue and swallowed. From his throat, he produced a low, guttural chant and closed his eyes, allowing the world to thaw into another.

When he next opened them, he found himself kneeling within a vast darkness. A darkness that churned and seethed as if the blackness was somehow aware of his presence, disturbed by the unwanted intrusion. It was not silent within the dark, for a perpetual reverberation swarmed the endless gloom. Kabad embraced the overbearing rumbling and turned his gaze to the boy's severed head.

'My Queen,' the Priest began. 'I speak to you from within the bowels of Kaer Kyral, the Kúnadman's lordly hovel. If you have means to speak, I would hear your counsel.'

For a long moment, there was nought but the lingering growl of the black, inky darkness, rolling with anger. But then there was a twitch, and the boy's features trembled slightly, a frown appearing upon the forehead with waves of convulsion. Flickering open, two foreign eyes revealed themselves, icy blue and familiar, searching the darkness before settling upon the Priest of Mórnos.

'*Kabad,*' the boy's mouth rattled, though the voice belonged to another. '*You have landed?*'

'I have, my Queen.'

'Good.' The voice was pleased. 'Soon we shall begin, and justice shall be the reward for our patience. Revel in this moment, Kabad, as it has lingered in our hopes for too long. Since the night your brethren were cast to the rocks, we have sought vengeance, and now, finally, we shall have it, with the death of the traitorous mongrels.'

'His death shall be sweet, my Queen,' the priest replied. 'I shall await the cover of night, and then I shall deal the justice owed our kin.'

'It is only the beginning, Kabad,' the voice said, eyes rolling back into the skull. 'Soon our justice will eradicate all who opposed the true king, and our justice will have no mercy!'

The priest smiled a smile of gold as thoughts of vengeance filled his soul and the voice of the queen silently embraced him.

The rain had waned enough during the last hour, that Ederys found a moment to leave her husband's side for a time and make her way to the Chantry. The old stone building was located on the northside of Kaer Kyral, on the edge of a short bridge, arching over a wide river that rushed towards the sea mouth. The water was rough, dangerous, and high. She had never seen the river so deep. Word had come from the east that the storm had raged across all southern Hyráeth, from Tenalír to Athíra. She thought the river might threaten to devour the bridge while she crossed and sweep her out to sea. In the end, she decided to assume it wouldn't.

Two Kúnadmen accompanied her across the bridge, along with two experienced war Kúnadi. The men were veterans of the rebellion, and both had seen the fall of Gordinal.

Malgwyn was a tall, wiry man with a curly red beard, streaked with grey. His companion was Skorn, a Kúnadi with patches of black and silver fur and piercing jade eyes, prone to snarl at the slightest noise or movement.

The Kúnadman to her right was Goreld, a gruff, stocky man, with white, wispy hair and a flattened wide nose. Prowling beside him, a greying Kúnadi named Rusk scanned the darkness. She was a pure breed, her back level with the Kúnadman's waist, marking her as one of the Kúnad Llían, companions bred in the Lord's Kennels. Such Kúnadi could live for a hundred years, maybe more, and were said to possess the blood of the Mothers.

Approaching the Chantry, they found the oak doors ajar, someone had also deemed the evening fit for worship. The Kúnadi, Skorn, appeared to flinch and back away from the entrance, sniffing the air and pawing at the ground. Rusk, on the other hand, was not so wary, panting impatiently as Goreld ordered her to heel, seemingly eager to enter.

'You smell something, girl?' Goreld asked, stepping towards the doors, his right-hand clenching around the hilt of the longsword that hung from his hip. Ederys had always found the stocky man overprotective, though she understood the benefits of such dutiful men.

'There's Kúnad Llían inside,' Malgwyn said, patting his companion. 'Skorn would submit to no less than the elder blood.'

'They'll be no need for that, Goreld,' Ederys said, placing a hand upon the pommel of the Kúnadman's sword. 'It's just one of my pups.'

She strode passed the two guards and entered the chantry.

Her footsteps echoed as Ederys stepped through the arched entrance and into the cavernous chantry. The pews to either side of the long hall sat empty, save for any lost spirits who lingered still. Above her, several stone gargoyles glared down, enveloped in feathered wings, mouths agape, baring unnatural, elongated tusks. They were forgotten idols of a fallen empire, an empire long dead, destroyed by the impious will of Mórddyn of Mórnos, and his ungodly heirs.

At the end of the hall, her eldest son, Prydonír, stood before the oak statue of the

Divine Maiden. At his side, the huge Kúnad Llían, Malíkhar, sat stoically. The Kúnadi's regal, silver coat, bristled in the draughty hall, his head rising as Ederys approached.

'Are you quite well?' She asked, her voice resonating throughout the chantry.

The Kúnadi's head tilted at the question and her son answered. 'I am well, mother... why do you ask?'

'So rare is it to find a child of mine in a house of worship, I judged you may be unwell.'

Prydonír moved his hand towards the stone altar that was the sculpted arms of the Maiden. Resting within her embrace lay Kaladwch, the Sword of Radiance, forged with silver and blessed by the druids of the old world. Her son's hand hovered over the blade, though he dared not touch it.

'Seize her,' Ederys urged, her son's head turning at the suggestion, and he frowned. 'Maybe you are the One. Maybe it is my son who shall be the Maiden's Chosen.'

'It is forbidden,' he said, removing his hand from the altar.

'Indeed, it is,' she said with a sigh. 'Although, it does seem odd. If no one can ever touch the damn thing, how will the Chosen ever be chosen?'

Her son's frown deepened.

'Well,' she said, reaching out to pet the Kúnadi's thick fur. 'If you are quite well and you seek not the Maiden's blade, why come here?'

Prydonír paused a moment before turning to face her. He had grown over the past year, his shoulders broad and strong. His hair was long and thick and reminded Ederys of her brother's, dark like the Háerlan truffles found by the domesticated Truffle Mochogs back home.

'What will happen if father dies?' he asked.

Ederys was taken aback. 'Do not say such things. Your father is in the hands of a Master Druid. They possess knowledge of healing beyond our understanding.'

Her son shook his head dismissively. 'You should not have invited him, mother. Father would not approve. It is dangerous.'

'You presume you know your father's mind more than I. This is no Priest of Mórnos or some dark servant of the black lake. Wórlyn is a Druid of Káer Dúsír, a man of peace.'

'It matters not which religious sect he serves, mother, the Great Lords will not approve.' He shook his head. 'Father spent a decade earning their trust, what will they think when they discover a druid has entered our halls?'

'You should not worry about such things,' Ederys said, reaching for his hand, which he refused.

'But I must,' he said sternly. 'One day I shall be Lord.'

'One day is not this day, Prydonír. Your father still lives, and he is more like to fight death itself than surrender to it.' Ederys took him by the arm. 'Let me worry about the Great Lords, I have dealt with their kind my whole life. They are not so scary.' She sighed as her son bowed his head, as if Ederys had lifted a weight from him. 'Tell me, have you seen your brother?'

'Rhodris?'

'No, Rhodris will be with the Kúnadmen. It's the little one who's hiding somewhere.'

'Ah,' Prydonír said with a hint of a smile. 'I believe I saw Jádyn and Elyssa sneaking into the library.'

'No?'

'Afraid so.'

Ederys shook her head. 'Little terrors they are. Come, let us find them.'

As Ederys, her eldest son, and his Kúnadi, left the Chantry, she glanced back at the Maiden, and thought she glimpsed a flicker of light.

Kaer Kyral's library was deathly quiet, save for the intermittent turning of a page. Jádyn raised a finger to his lips as Elyssa shuffled next to him, causing the wooden floor to creak.

'Shush,' he whispered.

Elyssa rolled her eyes and whispered back, 'he can't hear us from here, Jádyn. Can you see what he's reading?'

From their perch upon the library's second tier, the children's faces pushed through the banisters and peered down at the circular chamber. Sat alone at a round table, the druid, who had come to heal their father, was scrolling through a large, leatherbound book.

'I can't see,' Jádyn said, squinting.

'Maybe it's *The Black Cauldron*?'

'I don't think a druid would like children's stories,' Jádyn argued.

'Why not?' Elyssa asked. 'Children's stories are wonderful. They've got witches and monsters in them.'

Jádyn shrugged his shoulders, though before he could speak, a low, rasping voice arose from below.

'I am reading from the *History of the Lords of Dalkyr*.' Jádyn and Elyssa jumped at the sudden intervention. 'It is quite interesting actually,' the druid continued, 'though I must doubt the veracity of much of the author's claims. It is stated here that House Karanír served as kennel masters to House Brychán during the days of the Athirían Republic. This contradicts the oral accounts held by the druids of Dúsír, who state the House of Karanír were among the warband led by

Morddyn Bendráegol, who descended from the north.' He turned away from the book and looked up to the bannisters.

'Father says we have cousins in the north,' Jádyn said, noticing the druid's strange eye for the first time, ghost white, as if blind. His face was wreathed in blue woad that wound about his skin in tribal knots.

'Cousins you say?' the druid pondered. 'I suppose it is possible. Though it does beg the question, was it the northern line who migrated north, or the Dalkyrian line who migrated south? And who is the senior of the two?' He turned his pale gaze to Elyssa. 'What do you think, little one?'

Elyssa considered the question for a moment. 'Father says our family came here on the Maiden's Ships. If that is true, we landed in the south.'

The druid smiled kindly. 'If that is true indeed. Many noble houses trace their roots to the Land Before, but only the Druids of Dúsír can truly state such claims with any manner of confidence.'

'We have a Maiden Blade,' Jádyn argued, annoyed the druid would doubt his father's word. 'That means we came on the ships.'

The druid looked at Jádyn oddly for a moment and ruffled his brow before a smile gently returned. 'That is true, your family do possess a Sword of the Maiden, and I suppose that does grant some credence to the claim.' He raised his hand, also wreathed in woad, and stroked his sharp, red beard. 'Tell me, little lordling, have you or your sister entered the labyrinth?'

'You mean the maze?' Elyssa asked.

The druid grumbled and sighed. 'Yes. Though why people must change the names of things is beyond me.'

'We're not allowed in there,' Jádyn said. 'It's forbidden.'

The druid shook his head. 'A generation lost then. Customs and traditions forgotten. All for the folly of a mad king. There was a time when every noble son and daughter faced the labyrinth, that is how we found them.'

'Found who?' Jádyn asked.

But the druid's gaze was drawn to the library's wide doors. A few moments later footsteps could be heard approaching.

Elyssa took Jádyn by the arm and pulled him away from the bannisters. 'Quick, it's mother!'

Jádyn nodded and followed his sister into the shadows. They were good at hiding. Though seemingly not from druids.

Clunk!

Kabad drove his climbing pick into the slick, seaweed ridden stone of the Lord's Tower. The rains had come again, and such a climb was more than precarious. He rested a moment, finding a foothold with his leather boot and considered the violent waves crashing against jagged rocks far below.

A flutter of wings drew his attention as a black and silver raven approached from the north. The bird settled upon his shoulder and squawked.

'Away with ye, fiend!' Kabad declared. 'I have no want for your dark tidings this night. Go bother some other poor soul.'

'My Lord has bid me bother *you*, Priest of Mórnos,' the raven countered, shuffling her damp feathers. 'Our seers sensed your entry into Enún by way of the dead.'

'I had need to speak with my Queen,' Kabad explained. 'Now leave me be, Móriog. We seek no longer any guidance from the Azula.'

The raven cackled, seemingly amused. 'You speak as if *you* are who decides such things. The Priests of Mórnos have sought our guidance for a thousand years, without our knowledge, you would have been children lost in the dark.'

Móriog screeched as Kabad slapped her from his shoulder with some force. 'Where were the Azula when my brothers were stuffed into barrels and thrown to the dark waters? No, I think if your Lord could take away our power, he would have taken it long ago. Fuck you, raven, and fuck your lord.'

She squawked with indignation. 'Fool! My Lord will hear of this insolence, and he shall skin you alive!'

Kabad laughed. 'It is no more than I deserve, fiend. Now fuck off.'

'Beware the sun at dawn, Priest of Mórnos,' Móriog warned. 'For there he shall be, and so shall I.'

The raven beat her wings and flew away from the tower.

Clunk!

Kabad continued his ascent, his would-be destination, the dealing of death. As he reached the narrow window of the Lord's Chamber, he peered through the stained glass and found the Lord of Káer Kyral prone upon his bed, an old grey Kúnadi at his feet.

CHAPTER THREE

The Fortress of Kaer Kyral
Ádísday, 22nd of Voydych, 1005al

Two Kúnadmen with torches led Huwel towards the pens beneath the western tower, entering through an iron gate built into the face of the rock at its base. It had been a day since Ouric had failed to return to his post, and Huwel feared the worst. The rocks were dangerous on a good day, during a storm they could be deadly.

The Kúnadmen guided him through a damp, narrow corridor, eventually reaching a large chamber encircled by several Kúnadi pens. Beastly eyes peered through the iron bars, accompanied by panting and low growls.

'Do not stare,' one of the Kúnadmen warned, ushering Huwel out of the chamber. 'They dislike strangers, and I won't have them unsettled on my watch.'

Huwel nodded, averted his eyes, and followed his guides through another long corridor until they reached a wooden door. The Kúnadman knocked and waited patiently.

A moment passed before the door creaked open, revealing a short, stumpy man with thinning grey hair and small, round eyeglasses. The man was adorned with a white cloak that covered a brown habit. He looked at Huwel with an irritated look and then regarded the Kúnadmen.

'Well? Speak up man, what do you want?'

The Kúnadman cleared his throat. 'Friar Rhys, this guardsman here would like to speak with the captain.'

The friar turned back to Huwel.

'Is that so?' the holy man asked. 'A good many men would like to speak with the captain, though few seldom receive the honour. Might I ask why we should make an exception for you, guardsman?'

'I would like to report a missing person,' Huwel said.

'A missing person?'

'Yes. A fellow guardsman. Left his post and never returned.'

The friar's eyes widened, and he sneered. 'Abandoned his post without leave!? Quite appalling behaviour.' The stumpy man considered for a moment and then waved Huwel forward. 'Right, come on then. I suppose we can make some time for you.'

The room was teeming with the fog of piper's root, the smoking of which was a common pastime among men of dalkyr. Huwel himself had given it up a few years back, though the smell of it brought with it old cravings.

In the centre of the room, a long oak table was manned by several high ranking Kúnadmen, with the captain at its head. A tall and severe man, Captain Auríon was much respected and feared in Kaer Kyral. He was a bald man, though his black beard was long and full, albeit streaked with grey.

'There has been word from the Thane of Abermór, Captain,' one of the officers said, pulling a letter from his leather surcoat and placing it upon the table. He was a slight man with a long brown moustache and pug nose. 'It is stated here that a small band of warriors and several holy men arrived in the village a month or so ago and have yet to leave. The thane accuses them of disrupting the peace.'

The captain reached for the letter and read its contents.

'Have we any knowledge of this band of brothers, Sir Robír?'

'It is unclear, Captain,' the officer said. 'Could be the Híanna, but we cannot be sure.'

The captain frowned. 'As soon as this bloody storm passes, send men to investigate. If they're causing trouble, remove them.'

'Yes, Sir.'

Friar Rhys interrupted the discussions. 'Apologies, Captain, we have a guardsman here who would like to report a deserter.'

Huwel's eyes widened. 'No not a deserter-'

'A deserter you say?' the captain said, a single brow raised.

'I'm afraid so, Captain,' Friar Rhys said regretfully, though Huwel sensed his demeanour was feigned somehow.

'Abandoned his post at night and failed to return.'

'Maiden's mercy,' Sir Robír cursed. 'Who was this then?'

'Ouric, Sir,' Huwel answered warily, suddenly deliberating whether reporting the boy's disappearance was the right thing to do. 'A young lad,' he added quickly. 'His mother is worried sick.'

Friar Rhys shook his head. 'Such a shame. The carelessness of youth oft spawns dire choices. I suppose he'll have to be hunted down and disciplined.'

Amidst the murmurs of agreement from many of the officers around the table, Huwel was acquiring a growing dislike for the little friar. He only hoped Captain Auríon would see things differently.

'Ouric you say?' a voice spoke. Huwel turned his head and was shocked to find Rhodris Karanír leaning against the back wall. A tall lad with light brown hair, and the look of his mother about him. Shamefully, he had failed to notice the young lordling, and now felt awfully embarrassed having not bowed to the Lord's second born son as soon as he had approached the table.

'Young Lord,' Huwel said, bowing low. 'I apologise, I did not see you, my eyes are not what they once were and-'

The lordling waved away Huwel's concerns. 'I am no lordling here, only a Kúnadman. You said the deserter's name is Ouric?'

'Yes...Sir,' Huwel said, unsure of how to address the lordling. 'Ouric Singsong he is better known by in town.'

'You know the boy?' Captain Auríon asked of Rhodris.

'I do,' Rhodris said, approaching the table. 'He used to play with me and my brother when we were children. Ouric always dreamed of serving as a guardsman, I would not think him the type to abandon post.'

Huwel released a relieved sigh. 'That is true, Sirs, Ouric is a good lad,' he said, pleading. 'I fear something grave may have happened to him. I have searched the beach but there is no sign. His mother-'

'Have you searched the caves?' Rhodris asked.

'The caves, Sir?'

'When we were young, we would make dens of the caves,' the lordling said. 'A place to hide away and smoke piper's root, without my mother finding out.' He looked to the captain. 'The winds have been fierce of late. Ouric knows the caves well, he may have found shelter there. And with the tides high, he could be stuck.'

'Very well,' the captain said nodding to Rhodris and then to Huwel. 'Investigate the caves, see if you might find the boy. If not, we shall dispatch a search party.'

'Thank you, Captain.' Huwel said.

Rhodris Karanír strode from the table and urged for Huwel to follow. 'Come guardsman, I shall retrieve my Kúnadi and a few men and we shall search the caves.'

Huwel followed the young lordling and hoped with all his heart they would find the boy well, though he dreaded what they may discover.

Three swollen black leeches pushed and slithered their way up Madog Karanír's nose, causing the Great Lord's breath to quicken.

The Lord's Chamber swelled with the sweet-smelling aroma of incense cones that burned away in small stone bowls to either side of the lord's bed.

A pool of blood was forming upon the oaken floor, where the lord's Kúnadi lay dead, her throat cut. The old girl had seen the days of Ebonide Kings, and out of respect, Kabad had killed her swiftly. It would have been wrong to see the bitch suffer needlessly.

The Priest of Mórnos sat in the corner of the room upon a cushioned chair, stroking his long beard and waiting patiently for his little friends to do their work. In his hand, another leech wriggled about. He smiled at the creature.

'Let us see what the traitor has to say for himself shall we, Athanag?'

He raised the mórnosian leech to his nose and allowed it to enter. Sitting back in the chair, he let the blackness take him.

CHAPTER FOUR

The Fortress of Kaer Kyral
Ádísday, 22nd of Voydych, 1005al

The wintry night still roiled with wind and rain as several Kúnadmen trudged through the wet sand and seaweed, led by the young lordling and his female Kúnad Llían, Vórgarys. The Kúnadi was an agile beast with matted silver hair, who seemed to scale the slippery rocks, that littered the long stretch of beach, with ease.

'She looks at home, Sir,' Huwel said, catching up with Rhodris, who had paused to scan an area of long beach grass for anything of note.

'Vórgarys's father was a river Kúnadi,' the lordling said, clicking his tongue and pointing towards a jagged cliff face. The Kúnad Llían recognised her master's orders and headed in that direction, sniffing the air as she went. 'They like the wet and cold, and catching fish. If it rains at night, she'll scratch at the door until someone lets her out. She'd sleep within the eye of the storm if she could.'

Huwel admired the Kúnad Llían and wondered what it would be like to own such a beast. Larger and fiercer than the average Kúnadi, yet more loyal and trusting than the domesticated lizards they tame in the east.

'My brother was given a war Kúnadi on the day he was born,' Rhodris continued.

'Malíkhar,' Huwel acknowledged with reverence. Only the Great Lord's Kúnadi, Namorys, was more respected and revered among the peoples of Dalkyr.

'Aye, that's the one,' Rhodris said. 'Bloody thing thinks he owns the place. Struts about like a damned king. In many ways, Vórgarys is the far better Kúnadi. She's quicker, younger and the superior hunter.'

'I would not doubt it, Sir,' Huwel said, watching as Vórgarys bound across the encroaching tide, that left arcs of white foam upon the rocks. 'She is a fine Kúnadi indeed. Anyone can see it.'

It had been sometime since Huwel had walked so much, and as the group approached the caves, he was acutely aware that his right knee had begun to click with every step. It was quite audible, and he could only hope the young lordling hadn't noticed. He fiddled with his boot for a moment, trying to give the impression that it was the leather making the noise.

'Tell me, Huwel,' Rhodris continued. 'Did you serve during the rebellion?'

Huwel shook his leg and continued to walk with the lordling. 'I did, sir,' he said, looking to the young lad. 'Though I did not see much action, to be true.'

'Really?'

'Aye,' Huwel continued. 'My company was stationed upon the eastern walls of Gordinal, where the fighting never got to. Could see the whole thing from up there though. It was a bloody day.'

Rhodris nodded. 'You toss any barrels?' he asked.

Huwel dared not think back on it and suppressed the rising memories as best he could. The cruelty of what he had seen a decade past, was still horrifying to recall. 'I did not, Sir.'

There was a sharp bark then, and they looked up to find Vórgarys, haunches up, growling into the first of the nine caves that were gouged into the pockmarked cliff face. The Kúnadmen gathered around the entrance, along with three smaller Kúnadi, who mustered around Vórgarys.

'She's found something, Sir,' one of the Kúnadmen said drawing his torch towards the cave's black maw.

Rhodris reached out and patted the Kúnad Llían's back. 'Good, girl,' he said, calming Vórgarys, who continued to growl and bare her fangs.

Huwel stared into the blackness of the cave and shuddered. It was dark... far too dark. So dark he felt the deepness of the void could sweep him in.

'Come then,' Rhodris said. 'Let us enter.'

Huwel followed behind, as one by one, torches spitting, they stepped into the abyss.

Between the slopes of great rolling hills, Kabad made his way through a wide, rocky pass. In the distance, a warm light fell upon a small farmstead, where a lone man stood idle. There was a beating of wings and Kabad spotted a large, winged lizard, nestled within the crags of the eastern hill, its eyes fixed upon his own. He ignored the beast and continued, eventually reaching the tranquil farm.

He found Madog Karanír plucking crab apples from a small tree on the outskirts of the holding. The old Kúnadi Lord was dropping the fruits into a wicker basket at his feet, where a sheathed longsword lay.

'I have long supposed some may have evaded the Náedariad's Cull,' the lord said as the priest approached. 'Though I had not thought you one of them, Kabad Ydair.'

The priest laughed, 'I had not thought you a man of dishonour, Karanír. It would seem we were both mistaken.'

'You have come to kill me then?' Madog asked turning to face him. The lord looked just as he did when they had first met in

Gordinal. 'Come to sever my soul from its mortal coil?'

'King slayers belong not with the Blessed Mothers,' Kabad said mockingly. 'I shall send you to the void, where you will be chained with ebonide for eternity. The King trusted you and you stabbed him in the back, it is the least that you deserve.'

'Your brother was a vile fiend,' Madog said. 'He conjured his own fate. It just happened to be *I* who held the blade.'

Kabad spat and moved his hand to the pommel of his sword. 'I cut your Kúnadi's throat. The haggard bitch never saw me coming.'

Madog hurled something towards him and with swift action, Kabad drew his blade and cut it from the air. The riven crab apple fell to the ground and the Lord of Káer Kyral charged with his longsword held high.

The cave was dark and wet, and a foul smell lingered within. Kúnadman Gortheyrn knelt and held out his torch, illuminating the damp sand with an orange glow.

'Looks like something was dragged in here, Sir,' he said, gesturing to the disturbed sand. 'A small boat maybe.'

'What is that smell?' Another kúnadman, Rymon asked, covering his nose and mouth.

Huwel knew the smell and his heart sank. 'It is the smell of death.'

Rhodris looked him in the eye and then turned his torch to face the inner cave. The lordling drew his blade. 'Steel yourselves lads, we shall face what lies within. Send in the Kúnadi.'

Gortheryn stood and released a low, sharp whistle. Three Kúnadi, Vórgarys the largest of them, slipped further into the darkness. Rhodris and his men followed, and so did Huwel, warily.

Kabad and the Kúnadi's blades met as the priest managed to parry Madog's attack. Kabad spun his body, swiping the curve of his blade towards the Great Lord's neck. Unfortunately, a bulky fist caught him clean in the jaw and Kabad stumbled backwards. He was able to roll to the side just in time to dodge the falling longsword. The Kúnadi Lord growled as the blade struck the earth and Kabad threw a spinning kick into the back of his head, causing Madog to lose balance and fall to his knees.

Now was Kabad's chance, his chance for revenge. Ten years he had waited for this moment. Justice for his fallen brethren. He saw the lord's bare neck and drew back his blade.

'Goodbye, traitor!'

There was a screech, followed by a sharp pain that dug into the priest's shoulder. That damned flying lizard had assailed him and was now tearing through his cloak and clasping its claws into his skin.

'You are not welcome here, servant of Mórnos,' the lizard said, her voice stern. 'You will leave this soul in peace!'

The flying lizard lifted Kabad from the ground, digging her claws deeper into his flesh. 'Who the fuck are you!?' He bellowed, pain searing through his shoulder and neck. 'Release me!'

The lizard drew him further into the sky.
'As you wish,' she said, loosening her grip.
'No, wait!'
He fell and the ground met him with a thud that forced the air from his lungs. His soul swelled with pain and wroth, and he sought out the power of Mórnos to aid him. The Lord of Káer Kyral strode towards him with purpose and lethal intent, but the ground beneath them rumbled and shook as Kabad found the churning blackness within and brought it forth, his body rising from the dry earth, shrouded in a seething void of shadow.

Rhodris led the men into the opening where they discovered the small boat that had been hauled inside, bloody handprints marking its surface. Beside the boat, they found the remnants of a small fire, where the Kúnadi had found a pool of dark blood, soaking into the wet sand. A single iron pot lay turned on its side within the ashes. Huwel inspected the pot and found a layer of black paste coating the inside.
'What is this?' He asked.

The Lordling shook his head, a deep frown of concern upon him.

'Looks like some sort of ritual, Sir,' Rymon said. 'The Kúnadi don't like it. Something ain't right here.'

There was a shuffling of loose shale in the shadows, and all torches swung in that direction. The Kúnadi began to growl and bark at the darkness, yet Huwel could see nothing but damp, jagged rock.

'What the fuck was that?!' Gortheryn whispered, sword raised.

'It's nothing,' Rhodris insisted, though his sword was raised just as high.

Further shuffling came from another corner of the cave, and their torches spun to meet it. The Kúnadi ceased their barking and there was an ominous silence, an unnatural quiet, save for the moaning of the wind that swirled about the cave and stunk like rot.

The rocks before them were crooked and uneven, and Huwel had to squint to make anything out of the dancing shadows. Rymon dared to move closer, his torch revealing a shadowy figure hidden within the rocks. The

Kúnadman gently pulled back his blade and inched closer to the figure. Huwel and the others watched anxiously as Rymon lunged forward and sunk his blade into the rocks.

There was a clank and Rymon swung his torch forward. 'Nothing but stone,' he said turning back to face them with a smile of yellow teeth.

Rhodris and Gortheryn laughed with relief, lowering their blades.

'Thought there was a bloody ghoul in here,' Gortheryn chuckled.

Huwel did not laugh, as he saw Rymon's smile fade into wide-eyed horror and raised his weapon, pointing to the darkness behind them. Before they could react, a spear plunged through the back of Gortheyn's skull and emerged with his left eye hanging from the point, blood and gore sprayed forth, splattering across the Lordling's face and armour. Huwel froze as the Kúnadi began to bark once more and Gortheryn's body collapsed to the damp sand.

A headless figure moved into the orange light and the Kúnadi attacked.

The ground throbbed and ruptured, great scars swept down from the hills and tore into the pass. There was a great crash as a sink hole, a fiery void, swallowed the farmhouse whole.

Kabad, levitating above, embraced the ebonide mist that swirled about his being, and felt the energy imbue his soul with unnatural power.

He looked below and found the Lord of Káer Kyral on his knees in awe of the northern sky, where a vast black mass had formed, an ebonide serpent so huge it had blotted out the light of the sun, its gaping maw a void into nothingness.

The flying lizard that had assailed Kabad was perched upon a branch of the apple tree. It gazed up at the priest and met his eye. Kabad smiled before sending forth tendrils of dark power, that grasped the tree and tore it from the earth. The branches melted into the darkness, the apples decayed in mere moments, shrivelling into nothing. Leaves vanished and wood was vanquished, until the entirety of the tree was swallowed by the void. Madog Karanír could only watch as his reality was slowly engulfed by the ebonide mist.

Kabad descended to a lone tower of earth where the Great Lord knelt helplessly, surrounded by an eternal, black abyss.

'Maiden's mercy,' Madog whispered, tears in his eyes as he looked up at Kabad. 'What evil is this?'

The priest smiled kindly then, for in truth, this man was nothing more than a frail pup, oblivious to the hidden truths of reality. 'The Maiden has long departed this world, Lord Karanír, along with our Mothers. They have abandoned us.' Kabad gazed up at the great maw and its razor-sharp teeth that were as tall as the tallest towers of the world, and then back to the lord. 'Evil is but a construct of the human mind, as is Good. What was good a millennia ago, would now be considered evil, and what evil, good. They are meaningless.' Kabad held out an outstretched arm and a sword of black mist appeared within his grasp, the blade forged with voidstone. 'A man can only elect which path he will tread. I chose mine long ago, old friend.'

'What will await me?' Madog asked, his jaw clenched, though Kabad could smell the fear.

'Your soul will not return to the Mother's embrace,' the priest explained, and for this Kabad felt a flutter of sadness. 'Your crimes are too profound for that. Instead, your soul shall be taken to the void where you shall dwell for eternity. What lies there I cannot say, for it is beyond my knowing. But that is the path you must tread now.'

'My children...'

The voidstone blade fell upon the Lord of Káer Kyral, cleaving through his shoulder and scything down into his stomach. Radiant light bled from the Lord's body and the ebonide serpent's great maw descended to devour it.

'Rymon!' Rhodris howled, as the Kúnadi snapped and circled the headless figure. 'Rymon! Fucking pull yourself together and get over here!'

There was a yelp and a smaller Kúnadi was flung across the cave, its body snapped against the jagged rocks. Huwel rushed towards Rymon and pushed him into action. 'Protect your Lordling, Kúnadman!'

Rymon awoke from his shock and joined the fray, swinging his sword at the monster's side. The blade dug into the flesh, releasing a putrid stench. But the weapon seemingly did the thing no harm, as it reached out and took Rymon by the throat. Rhodris swung his sword and cut the arm from the body. Rymon fell free, only to be skewered by the spear that punched through his chest. The Kúnadmen let loose a horrible moan and he vomited blood.

There was another yelp as the headless thing's boot crushed the head of a Kúnadi. Huwel moved to pick up Gortheryn's sword and then grabbed the young Lordling. 'Get out of here, Sir!'

'What?' The lordling's eyes were wide, and his face drenched in the blood of his fallen brethren.

'This is dark magic,' Huwel said. 'It is a ritual of Mórnos. You must alert Káer Kyral. The Priests of the Black Lake have... ' Huwel paused a moment and looked Rhodris in the eye. 'There is a priest in the castle... with your family.'

'Maiden's mercy,' the lordling swore, and he raced into the darkness, leaving the cave.

Only Huwel and Vórgarys remained to battle the headless thing now. The Kúnad Llían was not so easily slain, and had torn chunks of flesh from the monstrosity, but had taken wounds herself, as blood dripped from her head where an ear hung loose. Huwel would not let the girl die alone, he rushed forwards and cut through the thing's leg at the knee. It toppled over still lunging with its spear, the weapon catching Huwel in the neck and blood sprayed. He reached up to grasp the wound, attempting to stop the blood. 'Fuck,' Huwel said. 'I'm done for now.' He fell to one knee as Vórgarys snapped and tore into the headless man, until eventualy the girl managed to pull the spear arm free from the body and deal a killing blow, and finally the headless ghoul fell lifeless.

In the orange glow, as the thing's writhing and twitching slowed, Huwel noted the guardsman's armour. He crawled towards the fallen body and grasped at the leather.

'No,' he cried, his words a razor. 'I... am... sorry, lad... I...'

Vórgarys was alone in the darkness, save for the dying breaths of an old man. *He was a good warrior,* she thought.

The glow of the torches soon faded and Vórgarys left the dying man to the darkness and sought out the last of the winter storms.

THE END OF PART ONE

Printed in Great Britain
by Amazon